silly Millies

It's a Beautiful Day!

Jean Haddon

illustrated by
Vicky Enright

Millbrook Press   Minneapolis

To Jon,
who makes
every day beautiful
JH

For Nogu and Pappa Bud—
for all that you do, thanks.
VE

Text copyright © 2006 by Jean Haddon
Illustrations copyright © 2006 by Vicky Enright

Millbrook Press
A division of Lerner Publishing Group
241 First Avenue North
Minneapolis, MN 55401 U.S.A.

Website address: www.lernerbooks.com

Library of Congress Cataloging-in-Publication Data
Haddon, Jean.
It's a beautiful day!/Jean Haddon; illustrated by Vicky Enright.
p. cm.—(Silly Millies)
Summary: Illustrations and easy-to-read text show that different weather conditions can mean "a beautiful day" to different animals.
ISBN-13: 978-0-7613-2834-6 (lib. bdg.)
ISBN-10: 0-7613-2834-3 (lib. bdg.)
1. Animals—Juvenile literature. 2. Weather—Juvenile literature.
[1. Animals—Habits and behavior. 2. Weather.] I. Enright, Vicky, ill.
II. Title. III. Series.
QL49.H274 2006   591.4'2—dc22   2003012056

Manufactured in the United States of America
1 2 3 4 5 6 - DP - 11 10 09 08 07 06

It's a
Beautiful
Day!

4

It is raining very, very hard.
Everything is all wet.
There are lots of puddles.

Whose mother would say,
"It's a beautiful day.
You may go out and play"?

A duck's mother would!

It is very, very cold.
Snow is on the ground.

Whose mother would say,
"It's a beautiful day.
You may go out and play."?

A polar bear's mother would!

It is very, very hot.
The sun is out.
The ground is very dry.

Whose mother would say,
"It's a beautiful day.
You may go out and play"?

A camel's mother would!

It is raining very, very softly.
The dirt is very wet.

Whose mother would say,
"It's a beautiful day.
You may go out and play"?

A worm's mother would!

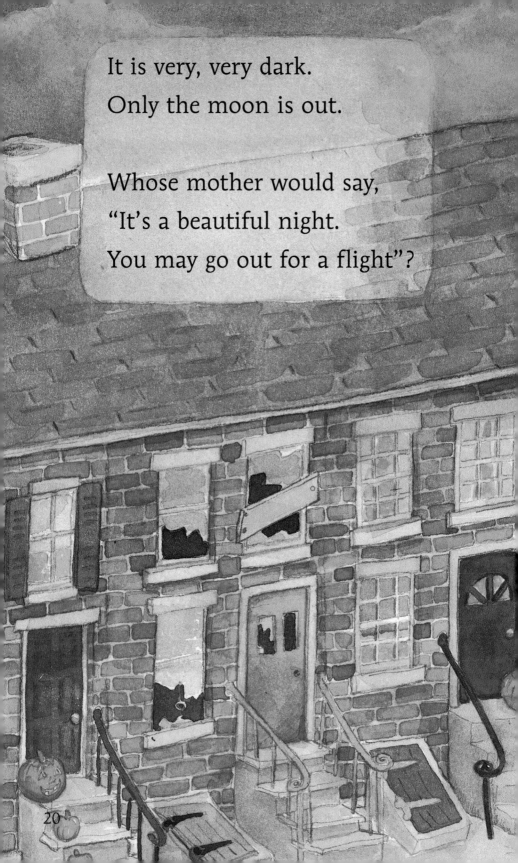

It is very, very dark.
Only the moon is out.

Whose mother would say,
"It's a beautiful night.
You may go out for a flight"?

A bat's mother would!

It is very, very windy.
The waves are very big.
It is a hurricane.

Whose mother would say,
"It's a beautiful day.
You may go out and play"?

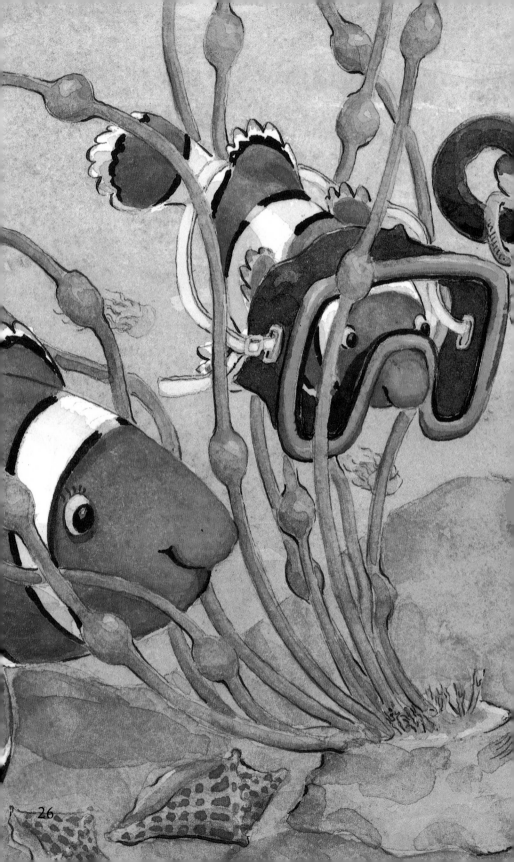

A fish's mother would!
(It is always quiet way
down under the water.)

The day is very, very beautiful.
The day is not too hot.
It is not too cold.

Whose mother would say,
"It's a beautiful day.
You may go out and play"?

Your mother would—
of course!

About the Author

Jean Haddon is the mother of three children who insisted on skiing in snowstorms, sailing in windstorms, and basking in the desert sun. Their attitude toward the weather notwithstanding, they all grew up just fine. Jean, however, bundles up for the cold of the Connecticut winter and wears lots of sunscreen in the summer. She is the author of two other Silly Millies.

Tips for Discussion

- It is important to search the pictures for clues about words. After you've read the book a couple of times, try to remember whose mother will approve of what kind of weather.

- Did you notice the footprints on many of the spreads? What do they tell you?

- Another picture clue: Find one main thing in each of the different weather pages that reappears in the following spread. *Hint*: Most of them are things to play with.

- Think about which season of the year each of these scenes might be taking place. What is the clue in the night scene, where the weather doesn't help you guess?